BARE
BEAR

Jez Alborough

ALFRED A. KNOPF • NEW YORK

THIS IS A BORZOI BOOK PUBLISHED BY ALFRED A. KNOPF, INC.

Copyright © 1984 by Jez Alborough
All rights reserved under International and Pan-American Copyright
Conventions. Published in the United States by Alfred A. Knopf, Inc.,
New York, and simultaneously in Canada by Random House of Canada
Limited, Toronto. Distributed by Random House, Inc., New York.
Published in Great Britain by A & C Black (Publishers) Ltd.
Manufactured in Hong Kong by South China Printing Co.
2   4   6   8   10   9   7   5   3

Library of Congress Cataloging in Publication Data

Alborough, Jez. Bare bear.

Summary: Rhymed text and illustrations reveal what the polar bear
has on under his familiar white furry coat. [1. Stories in rhyme.
2. Polar bear—Fiction. 3. Bears—Fiction] I. Title.
PZ8.3.A33Bar   1984   [E]   83-25119
ISBN 0-394-96808-5 (lib. bdg.)
ISBN 0-394-86808-0 (trade)

for Jenny

To keep warm in
the arctic air,

a polar bear wears
polar wear.

On his back a polar suit

and on his foot . . .

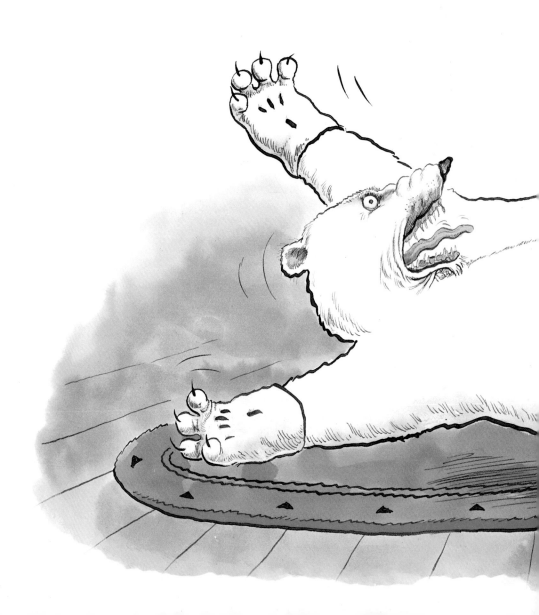

. . . oops! . . .

a polar boot.

His gloves are really

quite fantastic,

attached to him
by pink elastic.

His socks he changes
once a week:

no wonder all his tootsies reek!

Such a struggle

such a task

to pull away a
furry mask.

He zips his zip
and under there . . .

pale blue polar underwear.

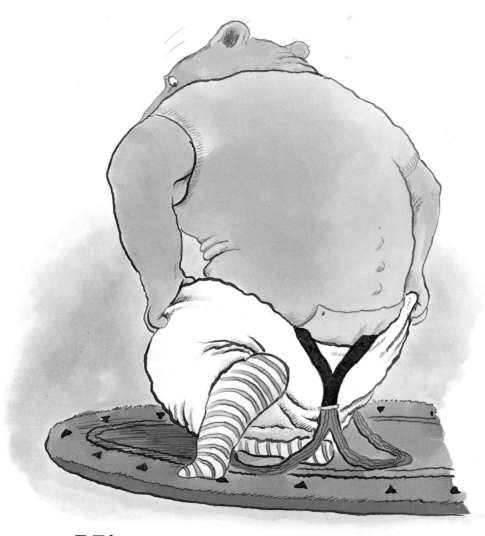

His trousers dropping
to the floor,

he tiptoes shyly
to the door.

And in the steaming bath
we find . . .

a great big, bulging
bear behind.